Bloodlust

Bonnets

First published in the United States of America by Andrews McMeel Publishing,
a division of Andrews McMeel Universal, in 2019

First published in Great Britain by Simon & Schuster UK Ltd, 2019
A CBS Company

Copyright © Emily McGovern, 2019

Interior colour by Rebekah Rarely

The right of Emily McGovern to be identified as author of this work has been
asserted in accordance with the Copyright, Designs and Patents Act, 1988.

1 3 5 7 9 10 8 6 4 2

Simon & Schuster UK Ltd
1st Floor
222 Gray's Inn Road
London WC1X 8HB

Simon & Schuster Australia,
Sydney

Simon & Schuster India,
New Delhi

www.simonandschuster.co.uk
www.simonandschuster.com.au
www.simonandschuster.co.in

A CIP catalogue record for this book is available from the British Library.

Trade Paperback ISBN: 978-1-4711-7895-5
eBook ISBN: 978-1-4711-7896-2

Manufactured in China

Bloodlust
&
Bonnets

by Emily McGovern

**SIMON &
SCHUSTER**

London · New York · Sydney · Toronto · New Delhi

A CBS COMPANY

PROLOGUE

Somewhere in Great Britain at the tail end of the Regency...

Of course the real problem is that we have too much land.

Mama insists we hire more peasants, but I see no sense in that.

More peasants, more problems—wouldn't you say, Miss Lucy?

. . . Miss Lucy?

May I see that a moment?

My cane? Certainly.

Handle is a touch weathered.

Still, sturdy old thing. Gets the job done.

Oh good.

BIFF

Miss Lucy?!

Whatever are you doing?

Something I should have done

A long

time

ago.

SH-INK!

HAAA!

I say! That woman has become hysterical!

Unacceptable!

Subdue her!

Gentlemen,

I do hope you like honey,

for I have a bee in my bonnet.

HAVE AT YOU!

lop

SWISH & MISS!

Huh?

BIFF

uh oh

SLICE!

DUCK

You fight well, girl.

One rarely sees such bloodlust in a girl of your standing.

Well. Active bloodlust.

Anyway, it all makes you a rather ideal candidate to join . . .

HA HA HA HA HA HA

my secret ancient immortal vampire cult!

Wow, really!

Yes

Now prepare yourself for . . .

YOUR INDUCT

-HRK

GASP

VII

I think that's all of them.

More will come.

Let us fly to my magic castle deep in the Scottish Highlands!

Are you hurt, Miss Lucy?

I have a poultice in my sporran, should you require.

Right now there's only one thing I require.

SMOG

Come, Napoleon!

We wish you to fly us to my magic castle deep in the Scottish Highlands!

I know.

I am psychic.

There's a good boy.

Finest bird in all Christendom!

Oh, Napoleon. What you 'ave become.

By the way, Lucy— awfully perceptive of you to spot those biters!

To the untrained eye they look just like respectable English gentlemen.

How did you know they were vampires before you began to slaughter them?

Um

It's . . . terribly complicated, Lord Byron . . .

I'll explain at the castle.

Right-ho! Onward, Napoleon!

Onward to Scotland!

Ahh, my magic castle deep in the Scottish Highlands! Gosh, it's good to be back.

Welcome home, sir.

Who said that?!

It's the castle! Magic, remember?

How are things, Castle?

All in order, sir. I trust sir's trip was productive?

Exceedingly so, Castle. Lots of dead vampires.

Oh good, sir.

This is Miss Lucy— my companion and fellow slayer!

Welcome, Miss Lucy. Is there anything I might offer you?

How about some fresh garb, old girl?

Certainly, sir.

One moment.

bing!

1

3

Ok, then, g'night!

Yes, sir.

Good.

Night.

SOME HOURS LATER...

Psst. Lucy.

Pssssst.

PSSST. Lucy.

Mrrnghh...

LUCY.

Aah!!

What you seek . . .

is in . . .

the library . . .

Mmwhere's that?

Follow meee . . .

That's it . . .

Mrgh

4

But—we exploded you!

You died!

Immortal, child!

IMMORTAL.

Admittedly, it was not the most graceful of exits.

But nothing I couldn't recover from, thank you for your concern.

And I still wish you to join . . .

my secret ancient immortal vampire cult!

Really?

Still?

Then let us resume . . .

YOUR INDUC

- HRK

Wha . . .

GAARK

HURP

MLAAAK

HNG THAT

DAMN

POET

Lucy, it is I! Lord Byron!

You know, from books.

Yeah, hi, Byron.

Gosh, what are the odds? Saving you again, in the exact same manner!

'Twas that dastardly lady vampire!

She's got it in for me, I tell you!

Stalked me halfway across the country just to take another crack at me!

Well, I showed her what for! I suspect that's the last we'll see of HER, whoever she was.

Gosh, I hate to think what might have happened if I hadn't arrived in the nick of time again!

Wait, look!

smoo *pooch*

In the viscera!

?

Her calling card!

Ah, a clue!

What is it? A jewel? A fang?

The Queen of Diamonds?

No, it's her actual calling card.

Got her address and everything.

Lady Violet Travesty
Vampire Towers

Absolutely DYING to see you! ~LVT
xxx

Good lord, how convenient.

Good morning, sir.

Castle! Did you see that? The vampire lady?

Yes, sir.

11

Ok, here we are, Vampire Towers!

Yes!

Got everything? Swords, garlic, crucifixes? Bloodstained calling card?

Yes!

By the way, did we bring our own calling card? To leave in case she's not in?

No.

But isn't the whole point to ambush and assail her? Won't the calling card throw that off a bit?

Oh yes. But. You know.

Important to do these things properly.

Anyway.

Remember the plan—we burst in, and you get rid of any acolytes while I run and overpower Lady Travesty using the garlic and crucifixes.

Then we can question her about the cult.

And, remember, it's important you don't get carried away and stab her again.

Right.

12

Cos she'll only pop up again somewhere else.

Right you are, m'dear. No stabbing!

All right, on my count . . .

One . . . two . . . three . . .

GO!!

POW

What was that?!

COUNTER AMBUSH!

Take cover!

Surrender now or the next one will blow your bonnet clean off!

How did they know we were coming?

They've got some kind of explosive device . . . our swords will be useless.

You're not a child! Who are you?

Are you a boy or a girl?

What are you doing here?

Sham, yes, and killing vampires.

Gosh, what a coincidence. That's what we're doing.

Have you seen a lady vampire? Rather large, pointy-looking, fangs and so forth, dramatic gestures?

Lady Violet Travesty. That's who I'm after.

Well, what luck! But I'm afraid we can't have you killing her, old chap. We've been through that rigmarole before.

Did you know she just pops up again somewhere else?

Only if you're dim enough to use steel.

Steel?

Obviously, you can't kill vampires with steel, only incapacitate them so they're forced to regenerate elsewhere.

Every vampire hunter knows that.

Well, yeah, obviously.

Obviously.

Anyway, we don't want to kill her or make her pop up somewhere else. We want to capture and question her.

Can't have you using this thing and killing her stone dead.

It won't kill her.

Hah! So you don't know how to get her either!

It's a modified blunderbuss loaded with a special mix of gunpowder and crushed garlic.

Enough to stun her but not kill her or allow her to escape.

Well, you . . . certainly have thought this through . . .

Too bad, now we've got it.

And sort of know how to use it.

Yeah

Look, I've got a suggestion I think will suit everyone.

SOME MINUTES LATER...

Ok, ready?

Ready!

Lady Travesty will be in one of the castle's inner rooms. I'll blast through the first wave of henchmen, then you two take on the rest while I run through and stun Travesty.

Then you join me, and we'll drag her out and put her on the bird—

Napoleon.

—sure, and we'll fly her to your place to interrogate her.

Now—on my count . . .

One . . . two . . . three . . .

GO!!

BAM

HAA!

Helluuu?

Napoleon, are you sure this is Vampire Towers?

I am psychic, not géographe.

Sham, there's no one here . . . Are we in the right place?

I followed the signs to this location . . . I could have sworn . . .

Don't shoot!

RUSTLE

Who's there?

Take anything you want! I'm unfathomably rich and successful!

Hang on . . .

I recognize that voice . . .

Hands up!

Aahh, please don't shoot me!

Who is it, Byron?

By God.

If it isn't my arch-rival, whose ill-deserved popularity I feel utterly unthreatened by . . .

. . . Sir Walter Scott

Byron!

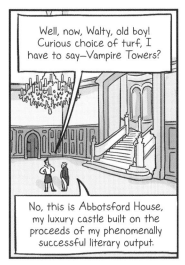

Well, now, Walty, old boy! Curious choice of turf, I have to say—Vampire Towers?

No, this is Abbotsford House, my luxury castle built on the proceeds of my phenomenally successful literary output.

Hmmm, Abbotsford . . . can't say I'd heard of it . . . but terribly nouveau and all that!

Course my patch has been in the family for centuries . . .

Oh yes, I do recall, such a delightful, crumbling old hovel it was. Very picturesque!

But with so much money rolling around—had to put it somewhere, what!

Oh, absolutely, old boy, absolutely!

Hahahaha

CLAP

HRK

Hahahaha HA

Uff

Ah ha haha

SLAP

HRK

HAAAAA

So what do you want to question Lady Travesty about?

Oh, you know, the cult. Vampires, etc.

What about you? Why are you looking for her?

It's classified. I'm a professional.

SOME TIME LATER...

God, I'm hungry. When's the last time we ate?

I have some biscuits in my sporran if you like?

Thanks.

* munch   munch   munch   munch *

So this Sham fellow—what are we going to do about her?

What d'you mean?

Well, we're a double act, a duo! Sham throws off our rhythm.

I didn't know we had a rhy—

I mean, what does she REALLY bring to the operation?

You mean apart from firepower, tracking skills, and professional vampire-hunting experience?

Yes, apart from that.

I think she's

you know

cool.

Pssht, WE'RE cool!

Look at us!

* munch   munch   munch *

27

Come on, Byron, have a bit.

I refuse! Barbary!!

So the new plan is to get to this baroness and ask her about where we might find Lady Violet?

Scott said she "associates" with vampires. She should be able to point us in the right direction.

So do you . . . hunt vampires full time, Sham?

You seem very . . . competent.

Well, I'm an expert. Best vampire hunter in Britain. Ask anyone.

How about you?

Um, well, I—

I'm a poet and adventurer!

Lady V seems pretty keen for you to meet again.

Oh yes, they're OBSESSED with me. Always springing up at inopportune moments! That's why we're on the hunt, to get the jump on her!

And when I'm not engaged in derring-do, I am, of course, a renowned poet.

Pfft

You disapprove, eh! Such is the poet's lot . . .

Anyone can string some words together and call it a poem.

Go on, then.

Oh, but I am/ a bird in a cage/ that you have put me in/ so I may sing for you/

but I cannot sing/ for I am in a cage/

the cage you put me in/

you are the cage/

it's you/

please let me out of the cage/ I don't want to be in the cage/

with you

Wait—they ARE the cage, or they put you in one?

Yes

But then why are they also in the cage?

Look, the point is, not everyone can sit around talking about feelings all day.

Feelings are a waste of energy resources that could be otherwise put towards completing the mission.

Speaking of which—wrap up that meat, it's time we were going.

Feelings are a waste of time? What tosh!

She seems to be right about a lot of other stuff, though . . . Let's maybe try not to have too many feelings about things, just while we're on this mission?

. . . I'm not sure how I feel about that.

Good work.

Come on!

29

SOME MORE DAYS LATER...

Ah, well. We're lost. Napoleon is incommunicado. We'll never find BB's place like this. I suggest we find a nice country inn, have a slap-up dinner, and chalk this one up to a victory!

What!

Who's "BB"?

We can't go back now, Byron! We're on a quest!

And we're not lost, I'm just . . . recalibrating . . .

Dear girl, the quest doesn't seem to be advancing, does it?

It would if you two didn't keep faffing around . . . making me stressed . . .

Don't be stroppy, Byron.

I am NOT stroppy, I am an enigmatic and unpredictable genius!

Now come, my love, let's go home. It's probably this way.

31

33

Well, Byron, how lovely to see you again! Feels like only yesterday I first discovered you disoriented and trespassing on my property!

Wonderful you keep up the tradition.

Jolly good to see you, BB!

And this time you've brought some bedraggled little friends! Charming, charming.

Err, hello, ma'am. Thanks for rescuing us.

Though, for the record, we were doing perfectly fine.

Not at all, my dear urchins. Welcome to my palatial home!

Do make yourselves comfortable.

Just kindly refrain from touching or sitting on anything.

Baroness—we're hunting a vampire by the name of Travesty. Sir Walter Scott said you'd know where to find her.

Urgh. Horrid little man.

Haha, yes, BB!

He said you, um, associated with her . . . kind.

How dare he.

Utter cheek.

Although . . . as it happens . . . I am attending a party tonight, hosted by a very stylish society lady who is of that . . . ilk.

Ooh, she's a vampire?

Yes, dear.

35

36

I wonder what the ball is going to be like.

We won't spend long there.

We need to get in, gather as much intelligence as possible, and get out.

Intelligence? Like what?

Anything to do with Lady Travesty or other vampires. Strategies, goals, traceable locations, strongholds, tactics.

All their most guarded secrets. And all while keeping our presence completely under wraps.

Crikey, how exciting.

Sham! Come help me a moment!

Get in, intelligence, strategies, strongholds . . . secrets . . . ok. Right. Sounds good.

Byron!

My love!

No, no, listen to me.

We need to be in top form tonight, ok? No blundering. We need to show Sham we can handle ourselves, yes?

Just . . . no feelings, no mistakes, ok?

Whatever you say, my sweet!

And stop all that soppy stuff. I feel like Sham is judging us.

So we're allowed to feel judged, then?

Yes, that's fine.

Come along, lovebirds! Time to get ready.

SOME TIME LATER...

Urgh, I hate short sleeves. I feel vulnerable.

GOSH, I look divine.

And, Lucy, you look lovely! I hardly recognize you!

Ready, Byron? Got your disguise?

Prepare yourselves . . .

Tah-daah!!

Oh God, really, Byron?

We're supposed to be low-key . . .

SOME TIME LATER...

40

Ooooooh, fancy.

Right, I'm going to go INFILTRATE.

snatch!

sluuuurp

flap
flap
flap

So . . . do vampires hate all poets? Or just Byron specifically?

I'm not sure, you know. Byron certainly seems to rub them the wrong way. He never was one to take a hint, unfortunately.

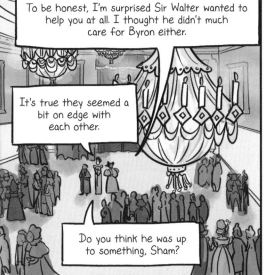

To be honest, I'm surprised Sir Walter wanted to help you at all. I thought he didn't much care for Byron either.

It's true they seemed a bit on edge with each other.

Do you think he was up to something, Sham?

41

It's possible. Can't trust anyone, really.

It's like I always say, "Why tell the truth . . . ?"

CHOMP

. . .

Oh, is that it?

Seems like he sent us in the right direction, though. And Lady Travesty will hardly be able to resist a gathering like this.

How come?

Vampires are all obsessed with showing off to each other.

That's always their main concern.

In the old days it was virgins and bloodthirst, but these days it's more about parties and dramatic gestures.

Everyone is trying to maintain their image and work out how to stay ahead of the pack.

Terrible people to work for, though.

Always coming up with crazy, convoluted plans to outdo each other. It's a nightmare to keep track of.

You worked for vampires?

Err. No. So I hear.

They DO know how to throw a party, at any rate. I hear our host is a FORMIDABLE woman.

A veritable "grande dame" of the undead social scene.

A "grande dame"?

I think it means "big lady."

Hush, here she comes!

Countess Gladys De Harridan herself . . .

Gladys De . . .

I thought you said this was a Travesty party?

No, no, dear—De Harridan! The most distinguished vampiress in all of London!

Now be quiet and try to look exotic.

I'm just going to, um,

step out for a minute.

Make sure the carriage is,

um . . .

Wow, she's scary.

The French tried to guillotine her, like, three times. The thing just bounces off her. They say she's indestructible.

They say the Scarlet Pimpernel tried to rescue her in 1793 and she called the police.

44

Hrrghh

Sham?

Byron?

I am afraid not, mademoiselle.

It is I,

Countess Gladys De Harridan!

Are you working for Lady Travesty? Take me to her!

I know she's the head of the vampire cult. She knows who I am, and she's going to be FURIOUS at how you've treated me!

Travesty? Pah!

Lady Travesty is not the leader of this social set.

So who is?

Voila

Oh.

So are you . . . are you going to try to induct me? Into the cult?

To what end?

Err, it's just—I mean, that's what Lady Travesty—

Lady Travesty is a pretender. She has no authority here! Her miserable excuse for a cult is but a pale imitation of the House of Harridan . . . I suppose she must look for recruits where she can find them.

In London we have somewhat HIGHER standards.

She said I was special.

That is incorrect.

Oh

I am curious, though . . . what was your plan, coming here with that man?

We were hunting Lady Travesty, and so we came here in DISGUISE to fool you all, and we were . . . we were going to . . .

We were . . . investigating . . . strategies . . .

Yes?

We were going to come here and get intelligence so that we could . . . um . . .

...

In retrospect, we should probably have discussed it a bit more. We just got carried away with the dresses and everything . . .

Regrettable.

But they're definitely coming to save me!

I think not.

The poet will die—

Why? Why are you so determined to kill him?

My dear, we would not give a fig for the affairs of Lord Byron, but he WILL NOT stop turning up to our parties with a sword and stealing all the attention.

He RUINED my speech, and now it's all anyone will be talking about.

What I would like from you is news of our dear Lady Violet . . . you will tell me of her plans!

Why does she pursue you?

There must be something she is seeking, some plot to undo me . . . I will winkle it out of you.

I won't tell you anything!

That is no problem, I have factored this stage into the interrogation process.

What happens now is I will simply torture you physically until you do so.

THWACK

What . . . what sort of information were you after, hypothetically?

What did she tell you about me? What lies and disgusting stories has she been spreading?

Err . . . I actually hadn't heard of you till tonight. She didn't mention you.

Not even once?

Perhaps she referred to me as GDH. Some people do this.

No. Sorry. Don't think so.

But, then again, perhaps you are not the most perceptive of creatures.

That little raven-haired friend of yours, for example.

Don't you think there is perhaps more there than meets the eye?

Just how much do you know about the dashing young Sham?

I—wait.

How do you know who Sham is?

BAM

Oh, how did you—

GUARDS!!

Hiiiii

HA!

HRK

Lucy!!

POW!

Bloody aristo scum!

Aren't you an aristocrat too?

No time, Lucy, RUN!

We need to make it back to BB's carriage and hotfoot it out of here.

I'll send a signal out to Napoleon, and we must fly back to the castle at the earliest possible moment!

Have you seen Sham? Or BB? We should go back for them!

No time, Lucy, no time! We shall have to accept their brave sacrifice in the manner it was intended!

CRRK

But Sham—Gladys knows something about her. She might be in da—

Sham! What happened?

Um, we escaped.

We were . . . about to go back for you guys.

As were we! We were coming to find you.

We . . . knew you'd be here.

SOME TIME LATER...

MEANWHILE...

Well, no signal. In that case I suggest we repair to BB's house for a bite to eat and pick this up in the morning.

Lead on, BB!

I'm dreadfully sorry, darling, I'll have to drop you off here.

As I was departing the melee, one of the other guests mentioned a disgustingly rich and decrepit widower who's hosting an even more exclusive get-together just around the corner. Poor dear—apparently, he's all alone in the world and positively afflicted with funds. I must dash.

What?

Can we come?

Oh no, my darling, I don't think so! This is rather more rarified company than the last, and tarted-up street rats simply won't cut it.

Vampires are one thing, but rich widowers are quite another— I'm sure you'll agree!

Diverting company as always, Byron!

Take care, my urchins!

Now what?

What I'm saying is if BB had only given me a bigger WIG—

Oh, the wig would have distracted them from the SWORD you were waving around?

I wouldn't expect you to understand the power of a well-chosen accessory, Sham—

Maybe if the wig had been big enough to cover your FACE—

Ok, shut up a minute, will you! Let's think.

Byron, still no reply from Napoleon?

No, nothing.

We need to go somewhere safe, somewhere we can hide out.

Ooh, my club is just over there!

Your club?

Urgh

They'll look after us!

Some of us, maybe.

Psht, it'll be fine.

Look, we need to stay vigilant.

Who knows who will be in that club?

The vampires could have spies there, and we don't have the energy for another fight.

Nonsense, old girl, the whole POINT of a club is that it only accepts the right sort of people! Anyway, Lucy and I are going.

Fine, I'll find Lady Travesty a lot faster on my own.

No, no—

WAIT.

Sham, don't go now, we've come so far! Let's just go to the club for a quick snack, just while we think about where to go next?

Please?

Snacks, you say.

SNACKS!

Come along, then! Right this way, chaps.

So you're just going to rock up to your club with a broadsword, dressed in a bloodstained ball gown?

Well, it would hardly be the first time, Sham, old boy!

57

SOME TIME LATER...

Ha'ing fum?

AND SO ...

munch

munch

munch

So . . . I got chatting to Gladys back there.

Uh huh

That is, she tied me to a chair and threatened to torture me.

Yikes.

Anyway, she mentioned you . . .

said something a bit cryptic about how there's more to you than meets the eye.

Weird.

Does she know you?

She probably meant a different Sham.

Right.

So . . . you never said why you're hunting Lady Travesty.

I mean, obviously, it's great to have you along, but . . . what are you going to do with her?

Oh, you know. Ask her some questions.

Nothing for you to worry about.

Questions?

What questions?

What sort of questions do YOU want to ask her?

Um, well . . . I suppose she said something the first time we met.

Something about how I have a unique potential.

Which, obviously, yeah, I definitely do . . .

But it'd be nice if she told me precisely what that potential involves . . .

just so I'm clear on what my . . . "thing" . . . is . . . like, what I'm good at . . .

Um, aside from being super strategic and good at executing missions, obviously.

And then, after, I'd, you know, kill her or whatever.

You get it, right?

Oh sure. It's hard being so practical and efficient.

People admire you, but they don't get how tough it is, you know.

Yeah.

Exactly.

Anyway, like I said, I'm great at planning and strategy and stuff. But lately I've been thinking it'd be, I dunno, interesting to have, like, a partner—

Oh

Oh, excuse me, I—

Sorry.

No, no, it's my—sorry.

Um, so, as I was saying—

LUCY!

Ooh, skulduggery in the pantry, is it!

What are you two whispering about?

Talking about me, I'll wager!

Don't tell me, I won't hear it!

But, seriously, what were you saying about me

Nothing, Byron, we were talking about the mission. Go back to your party.

Thank you, dearest, I will!

I'm actually in the throes of poetic rapture. It's a shame you're missing it!

The similes are flowing like . . . well . . .

Like a fastly flowing thing!

Do you know

I remind me of a young meeee . . .

63

64

What the hell happened?!

Drugged. Or poisoned.

Where's Byron?

BYRON!!

Sham, he's gone!

What are we going to do?

Hold on.

Let's think.

Ok—first we need to get out of here, it's not safe—

SHHH!

Did you hear that?

CRRK

rrrrrrr

You called?

I am afraid not, miss.

I have not seen His Lordship since he departed on his quest.

Dammit!

Oh, this is Sham. She's helping us with the mission.

And is it Mr. Sham or Ms. Sham?

No

I see. May I take your coats?

Wha—

Thanks, Castle.

So let's hear your plan, then. Byron's not here—obviously—so why did we come?

Erm, that's the most . . . brilliant piece of my strategy . . . it's a safe place!

Sleep is a very important part of any well-thought-out mission.

Yes, that's it.

Allow me to guide you, miss.

The castle can find us some beds, can't you, Castle?

You . . . you are the REAL Castle this time, aren't you?

Oh yes, miss.

The "real" castle?

Yeah, last time we were here, Lady Travesty managed to bewitch and impersonate it.

I thought you said this place was safe.

Well, when you put it like that, um . . .

It'll be fine this time, won't it, Castle?

Oh absolutely, miss.

All this heavy stuff on the walls too . . . you're just asking for it to fall on someone.

Yeah . . . there's also a lot of weird magical stuff lurking in the grounds, apparently.

Just stay on high alert about everything at all times and we'll be fine.

I'm always on high alert, Lucy. And I'd've thought Byron would live somewhere a bit fancier.

I would have thought uninvited guests would appreciate staying in a magic castle for free.

Here we are.

Look, Lucy, if Byron's not here, we've no reason to stay.

We've been acting sloppily, making mistakes.

We never should have gone to that club.

Or the ball.

And, obviously, I'm completely in control but . . . remind me why we went to BB's again?

It's all part of the plan, Sham!

Something will come up! Definitely!

There's something special about this place . . .

Thank you, miss.

I—you're welcome—I just . . .

I mean, it's Byron's home, plus Lady Travesty did come here to the castle—bewitched it, took over its voice—

That was a one-off, miss.

There will be categorically no ethereal shenanigans this time.

Probably.

Yes, yes, I know, it's just—

DAMMIT, this knot.

Ok, ok, calm down. It's fine.

We'll stay here tonight and revise the plan tomorrow.

Here, let me.

Oh

smoooch

Um

Oh, I—

Um

I'm sorry.

It's fine.

It's just—when we were in the pantry and we both reached for that piece of bread—

What?

I thought you migh—

You know.

Like girls.

SOME TIME LATER...

Can you help me?

Oh. Who are you? How did I get here? Did I sleepwalk again?

I know not, child! I myself sought refuge in this forest while fleeing a band of brigands!

Brigands?

Brigands!!

They call me Gwendolyne. You are of the castle, are you not?

Yes—well, I'm staying there. The castle belongs to Lord Byron.

He's gone missing though. You haven't seen him, have you?

No child . . . oh, what a fate has befallen us all!

Something strange is afoot . . . a hidden power moves in the shadows and interferes with us . . .

Oh God, again?

Come, I am weary! Let us sit on the forest floor and tell each other tales of woe!

Um, ok

79

Lord Byron, he is a great poet, yes?

Oh yes! I mean, I think so.

And you are his companion?

We're working together. On a mission.

You are assisting him on a quest?

He's assisting me.

I see! And how has he assisted you thus far?

He, well, he—

He has . . . stabbed a couple of people.

Though his timing is

not the best.

My stars, and he has gone missing? You must be bereft!

Yeah . . . although he has been kind of a handful lately.

And he ignored me at the club.

And now Sham is angry with me, and it's all his fault cos if he hadn't disappeared, I wouldn't have panicked and made us come up here.

Sham? But who is this Sham?

Ooh, Sham's my other sidekick!

She's great.

We're an amazing team.

Though I did try to kiss her just now and she ducked.

Haha!

So funny.

Indeed?

But there was DEFINITE chemistry between us in the pantry, you know?

Mm, yes

Like we both reached for the same piece of bread and our hands touched, but it was more than just a piece of bread, it was what the piece of bread REPRESENTED—

Yesss, of course, my dear, I can tell your friendship is true.

Yeah!

That you trust her with your life.

That you have absolutely NO lurking suspicions about her.

Yeah.

Although.

It's POSSIBLE she might be hiding something.

Gladys De Harridan knew her name.

And she never quite answers my questions.

Also her motto is "Why tell the truth . . . ?"

Anyway

It actually doesn't matter cos I've got a secret too.

A secret?

How intriguing.

Yeah, I'm on a quest to find a vampire lady who recognized my true potential and wants me as her right-hand woman in a super cool vampire cult!

She chose me.

And soon I'll be a glamorous vampire doing glamorous vampire things, and that'll show 'em.

That'll

That'll . . .

Wow, how long have I been talking?

I probably should be going—

NO!!

You must stay with me, Lucy . . .

Tell me more about you, you are SO fascinating . . .

RIGHT?

I'm a spirited young lady flouting the gendered expectations of her time, but in a cute way!

I'm gonna go find Sham and explain it to her—

WAIT

Err

I . . . I must unburden myself of these bespoiled garments!

Ahhh, that's better!

Uh

I suppose I could stay for a bit.

Tell me morrre, Lucy . . .

Feed me your woe, let me gorge on it . . .

Well . . . I thought I was picking up all these signals from Sham, but now I'm wondering if maybe I'm just not very perceptive.

Reeeeeally?? What gave you that idea?

I dunno, it's more of a feeling than anything.

Though I'm supposed to be cutting down on feelings at the moment.

You know, in some ways I think it all relates back to my childhood—

Ok, that's enough.

HRK

Now, fair maid, I have you under my spell!

So I may draw out your soul and eat your life force!!

Too long have I languished in this forest, praying for someone to release me from my torment!

But now I shall take your place, and all that is yours shall be MINE!

Byron, the castle, the quest . . . I shall have it ALLLL!

You cannot resist . . . you will not . . .

Helluuu?

Who's there?

uf

?

RUSTLE

Oh, hullo, chaps.

Byron? What— how did you get here?!

What . . . what's going on, Lucy?

Why's there two of you?

What?

You—you're beside yourself!

That's not me, Byron, that's a magic demon thing! I'M me!

No, Byron, I'M Lucy! Don't listen to her, SHE'S the demon!

I . . .

What! Byron, is that a gun?

Where did you get that?

Leave her, Sham, she's just a weird demon with a crush on me.

Demon?

Crush?

Yeah, she was all over me, asking me about my life, you know.

Ah, well, that was—

Took her clothes off, tried to seduce me and everything.

Really?

Really.

Yeah, she says I'm fascinating.

Heh

Well, that was all part of the spell—you see, I'm a forest sprite, but I've been searching for a human vessel to possess and walk the earth devouring all I encounter, and Lucy here really was the most susceptible wretch I've ever had the fortune of encountering—

What was that, Sham?

What?

You said "heh"

in a tone that implied skepticism.

Suggesting you think I'm not fascinating.

Mm?

Not that I care whether you think I'm fascinating.

I don't.

I just want to clarify

that some people

do.

Cool.

Look, chaps—I'm sure there's a perfectly reasonable explanation for all this! The forest, the gun, me traveling hundreds of miles while unconscious, the succubus lady.

But what's important now is that we all get in out of this chill, back to the castle for a hot cup of cocoa, and—dash it all—a splash of laudanum, let's treat ourselves!

But we still don't know how or why both of you ended up in the forest in the middle of the night—

What were YOU doing in the forest in the middle of the night, eh, SHAM?

Pretty suspicious you just happened to find us, no?

Actually, I was out looking for you. I wanted to talk to you.

Oh

About what?

It doesn't matter.

I don't . . .

Sham?

I'm glad you're ok.

Err

Oh, LUCY, you can't IMAGINE what it was like to wake up all alone in this terrifying forest!

Actually, that happened to me too, Byron, remember?

Ah, well, anyway, back to the castle! Coming, Sham, old chap?

No, I'm going to stay out here for a bit.

Ahhh, this is just the ticket!

Hot cocoa, warm bed, good company!

Come on, Byron! You need to try to remember what happened. Think!

How did someone manage to get you all the way up here? Napoleon was with us—

I'm going to give him a stern talking-to about working hours!

Just as soon as he turns up again.

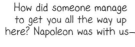

So whoever took you must have a similar ability . . .

Some magic to draw you up here . . .

Maybe it IS a trap and Lady Violet is going to come here! She's done it before after all.

Gosh, I hope not.

Tiresome woman.

Mmm . . . still, it's tricky, isn't it?

Cos, on the one hand, vampires are obviously bad and not to be trifled with . . .

Hear, hear!

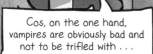

But, on the other hand, they are very glamorous and fancy and probably wouldn't cluelessly ruin your plans or give off confusing signals or keep secrets from you . . .

Though, on the third hand, vampires might not come rushing into a forest to save you from an evil, sexy succubus lady . . .

95

Well, I've got to say you've got a nice setup here, Sham! These two must be a good influence on you!

Uh huh

So did you two work together long, Virginia?

Not long enough! We were an amazing team. Best time of my life!

What with my other line of work going bust and that.

What line of work was that?

I was a highwaywoman, Lucy! Retired now, though. Tough business, you see. Not the style these days.

People don't find it so charming anymore when you put a gun in their face and take all their money.

Why's that?

I blame the economy, Luce. Nobody wants to have any fun.

The dandies back in the '90s, they LOVED a cheeky bit of armed robbery! Took it in the spirit it was intended, you know?

Anyway, that's why I came up to find ol' Sham here! Get the partnership going again.

And I'm looking forward to it now that you seem so relaxed, Sham! Honestly, I've never even seen you have a drink before! Normally, it's all "I'm working" this and "Focus on the mission" that.

Uh huh

Soon you'll be just like me!

Mmm, stop.

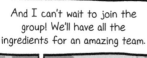

And I can't wait to join the group! We'll have all the ingredients for an amazing team.

You have to know exactly what your skills are and how to apply them.

You've got to be secure in your role and never be worried about being edged out or not being the center of attention.

And, naturally, you need to be comfortable with the fact that you'll make mistakes, and that's all part of growing and learning together!

And, needless to say, TRUST is the most important factor of all! Honesty and trust, foundation of good teamwork.

You three are totally in sync with each other, I can tell!

No secrets or lies, no secret misgivings or ulterior motives. Just 100% harmony and selfless devotion to the team!

...

LET'S DRINK.

YEAH!!!

Do I look old, Virginia?

Mrmf?

I found a gray hair, Virginia. GRAY.

You know who else has gray hair, don't you?

W...W...Walter Scott...

Nah, you're not old, Byron.

You're just saying that!

If I shot you in the face right now, the papers would say you died "tragically young."

You're TRAGICALLY YOUNG, Byron.

...I always could count on you, Virginia, old chap...

Yeah

AND LATER...

Nice sleeve.

Oh yeah, Castle made it for me, from Byron's dress.

Kind of silly for me to rip it off in the first place...not sure why I did that...

It's so cool to meet your old partner!

Well, "partner" is maybe a slight exaggeration.

I let her follow me around now and again, but I would never team up with her for real.

Why not?

She's a liability! Makes poor decisions, convinces me to go along with them. Follows pointless leads, causes distractions.

Before I knew it, I'd always end up tangled in one of her weird schemes and suddenly think, "Wait—what am I doing here?"

But—that's not what this is! Cos we've got a plan!

The plan is . . . wait, I've got it . . . the plan was, come to the castle, get . . . Byron . . .

I know! Now that we've got Byron back, we can definitely make him remember what happened back at the club. That'll be our new lead!

GOOD LORD, this whisky is good! Do you know, I can't recall a single thing that has ever happened to me! I feel like a newborn baby foal!

SHUT UP, BYRON!!

See how we bicker, Sham? It's all the unacknowledged sexual tension.

NO, BYRON, YOU'RE JUST REALLY ANNOYING.

THE NEXT MORNING...

Err. You off somewhere, Sham?

Oh!

You're up.

Yeah . . . I said, remember? Just one night here.

Oh, ok, I didn't realize you meant literally ONE night.

Hold on, I'll get my stuff.

No—wait!

Um

I'm going on my own.

I'm leaving.

On your own?

But . . . what about the mission?

I work better alone. I'm sorry, I shouldn't have joined up with you in the first place.

But—what about the team?!

Ooof, it's a rough one.

Yup

Did Sham sneak off at dawn, then?

How did you guess?

Her signature move, that.

Still, I thought she might stay this time! Seemed like she liked you guys.

Apparently not.

Ah, don't take it to heart. Happens to the best of us.

Anyway, seems like you're now definitely in the market for a new team member—we should join up!

I'm looking for a change of employment myself. I could help you on your mission quest thing! What's the project?

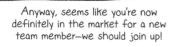

Urgh, I don't even know anymore, Virginia.

It all started out so simply!

Now I've got no idea who's doing what or why . . . I'm so confused . . .

Aw, now, don't cry, love!

You think YOU'VE got it bad—just wait till Lady Violet hears I've messed up her plan. She's gonna be FURIOUS!

What.

That is.

Err

Go out and stop her from leaving—tell her that Virginia is working for Lady Travesty and she needs to come—

Who is working with what?

Just—

Just stop her and tell her I need help, ok?

Urgh, oui.

Castle!

Yes, miss?

There's an intruder here, and I need you to help me capture them!

Indeed, miss.

So . . . can you do that?

What sort of thing did you have in mind?

I don't know—drop something on their head, anything!

What should I drop, miss?

Something HEAVY.

Yes, miss, absolutely miss.

Ok!

SH-INK!

Oh God oh God oh God oh God

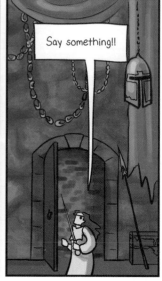

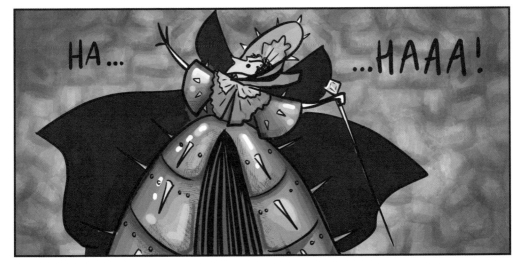

113

You!

Yes, "me," etcetera.

I would do the prelude, but we're a little short on time today.

We've doubtless only minutes till that kilted twit staggers in and delays us again.

Did you like the iron maiden dress reveal? Tricky to set up, but the payoff is always worth it.

And it has pockets!

What did you do to Byron?

Hardly a thing.

He did most of the work himself, just needed a little extra to tip him over.

You told Virginia to kidnap him and abandon him in the woods—why?

. . . Virginia did what?

I . . .

Virginia's methodology can be at times . . . opaque.

Interesting.

But no matter!

I have you ALONE, and now we shall—

Wait wait wait! I have more questions!

I met Gladys De Harridan— she said you're not a cult leader at all, that you're a . . . pretender!

HA! That crone.

114

JEALOUSY, Lucy. So transparent.

That woman is crumbling into irrelevancy, and she knows it. She'll do anything in her attempt to curb my ascent!

But, come, we'll discuss it on the way to Vampire Towers.

Err, actually, I've . . . since reconsidered.

I've got a team now, with Sham, and I'm, um . . .

. . . here to capture you.

Indeed? Strange, I thought I saw her leaving.

Something about how you're a burden and she wished she'd never met you?

She said that?

But, no, have it your way— I'm sure drifting around with a drunk narcissist in a crumbling castle is more appealing than joining a SECRET VAMPIRE CULT.

Farewell, then, Lucy, all the best.

No—WAIT!

Yes?

Um, aren't you going to try to persuade me a bit more?

Corrupt me with a big speech?

A speech?

Like, a big, dramatic speech about how I need to embrace the debauched and bloodthirsty side of my character and abandon my friends because you don't have to worry about pointless tiffs or forming complex relationships when you're too busy cackling and being glamorous and exacting wanton violence while cackling some more . . .

Ok, I'm back on board again! Let's do this!

Oh, fabulous!

Onward, then, to Vampire Towers! Where we shall—

Oi!

115

CHAPTER VIII – BATH

Come on, Virginia—give us SOMETHING.

What was Travesty's plan? Where's she going next?

I don't know!

Just tell us everything that happened from the club onward.

Well, she . . . she asked me to do some work.

She said go wait at the club for you and take the one in the dress up to Scotland, leave the other.

So I put the sleepy stuff in the champagne.

But then I got thirsty, so I had a little drink while I was waiting.

I stood guard, waiting for the right moment.

z z z z z z z z z z z z z z

I must have got distracted for a minute, cos when I looked up, all the men were on the floor. Apart from Byron—he was somehow still standing.

So I gave him a little bash on the head and did the special magic travel thing to get him up here.

SPECIAL MAGIC TRAVEL THING

But then at the castle I realized I'd got the wrong one, so I put him in the forest for safekeeping while I tried to think . . .

121

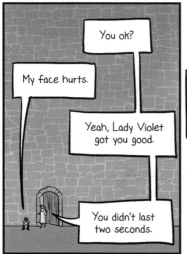

No, Lucy! I'm not taking this lying down—we have to go get her! We can't just wait around for her to lay another trap and ambush us again! We have to show her!

What should we do?

I don't know! But we can't just sit around doing nothing or hope that some huge clue just falls out of the sky!!

A letter came for you, Sham.

Apologies for the interruption.

Didn't care to interrupt when there were people breaking into the castle, Castle?

I do apologize for that, miss.

It would seem the intruder alert system failed.

What's the intruder alert system?

. . . Me noticing things.

Great.

It's from BB!

"My dear urchins . . . blah . . ." OH, listen to this—

"Whisperings of a singular set who convene in Bath . . . Lady Cronelia, a doyenne of the quadrille circuit . . . highly secretive . . . perhaps worth investigating yourselves . . ."

That sounds legit, right?

It does?

Sure!

"SINGULAR set..." Lucy, that's got to be Lady Travesty!

I guess... although last time BB's info wasn't, you know, completely accurate.

Nah, it's different this time, I can feel it.

It's got to be, right?

I mean, it's the only clue we've got! So it HAS to mean something!

Would I be talking about it so much if it didn't?

I guess I can't argue with that logic...

It makes total sense!

Ok, admittedly I haven't slept in days and just got my face smashed in with a stick, BUT—

Going to the wrong castle, joining up with you guys, coming to Scotland for no reason, running around this castle shooting ghosts, getting drunk, leaving you guys forever, coming back again, getting knocked out by Lady Travesty...

It all led to me being in this room so I could get a letter from an inconsistent source about something that MIGHT have something to do with the thing I was originally looking for!

You see??

I mean, what's more likely— THAT or the idea that I've been consistently misjudging things and making irrational mistakes?

I mean, I lost you somewhere in the middle of that, but I LIKE your energy!

Let's go to BATH!

YEAH!!

CLAP

I'm going to go tell Byron!

sniff

... Can I come?

Helluuu? Byron?

You ok?

Mmph

I could have taken her. Lady Travesty.

Sure.

She gave me that drink! That's a low blow, offering a chap a nice drink like that . . .

Yeah . . .

The thing is, Byron, we do still need to find her again if we're ever going to resolve this . . . quest.

You know, the thing we were originally doing, at the start.

We're still doing that?

Urgh, I'm so tired of it, Lucy. I just want to relax.

whump

Can't we just stay here and say we won?

No problem! You stay here.

Sham and I are going to Bath, to—

Bath?

Yes, BB sent us a new lead. Lady Violet is in Bath.

Probably.

Well, why didn't you SAY so!

A restorative trip to the spa is JUST what I need!

When do we leave?

Do have a seat.

Lady Cronelia will be with you in just a moment.

So, who is this lady?

I don't know exactly, but BB says she's the "doyenne" of the "singular set" she mentioned.

She'll know how to get us to Lady Travesty.

Really? BB said that?

It was all implied, Lucy.

Gotta read between the lines.

Ok . . . by the way, did you get any sleep yet?

No sleep!

On mission. Gotta do it.

One and done, Lucy! This is it! I can feel it.

Travesty in the bag, mission success!

Well, you seem very alert.

Gotta get it done, Lucy.

It's all going to pay off. It has to!

And then we can go join Byron at the spa!

Shh, someone's coming!

Dear guests! I am Lady Cronelia. Do forgive the delay, I was . . . otherwise engaged.

How may I be of assistance?

126

Good evening, ma'am. Perhaps you can help us.

We're looking . . . that is to say, we're on the search for a . . .

"Singular set."

IF you know what I mean.

I beg your pardon?

What my companion means is that we were sent here by a very reputable gentlewoman, with the assurance that we will find a certain

SINGULAR sort of society . . .

Oh . . . indeed? Well, my dears, it seems you have come to the right place!

You needn't say any more. I understand you perfectly.

Oh, great.

MANY fine young ladies and bachelors come to us in pursuit of our SINGULAR social opportunities . . .

Bachelors?

You mean like . . . ELIGIBLE bachelors . . . ?

Follow me, my dears. You have arrived just in time.

Yesss, this is it!!

127

The Bath Gavotte and Quadrille Club!!

Wha— . . . quadrille? Like a dance club?

EXCLUSIVE dance club, my dear!

A showcase of the cream of Bath society!

So . . . it's a dance club that acts as a front for the vampire cult, right?

Beg pardon?

Vampires! Lady Travesty! That's what all this is about, isn't it?? Otherwise what was all the blood oath stuff for?

My dear, it's standard dance club practice these days!

Even Almack's has a blood oath.

Wait . . . just to be clear, Lady Cronelia . . . is this really just a club for dancing?

Oh no, my dear, not at all!

Oh?

On Tuesdays we play bridge.

NGH

Come along, everyone —it's time to begin!

Places, places!

129

Come on, you two!

What—

It's the jig next!

Err

Oh . . . kay

So . . . it's just a dance club.

. . . What'll we do now?

I dunno, Lucy.

Maybe we should just go to the spa with Byron.

Who knows, maybe Lady Travesty will be there.

I mean even undead monsters need to relax sometimes, right?

Yeah, to refurbish themselves.

You know, after they explode.

You look like you could use some refurbishing yourself, Sham.

Yeah, I feel

Very tired.

TWIRL!

Hang on.

Sham?

Course I haven't had time off in YEARS. This is a work event for me.

Quadrilles are always full of feuds and conspiracies.

I'm just waiting for a wealthy socialite to give me a commission.

So I take it your mission to catch Lady Travesty isn't going well, then?

How do you know about that?

Heard there's a pretty big reward in store for you too. If you catch her, that is.

I have to say, it's taking you awhile. Do you even have a plan of action?

Of course I've got a plan.

See that girl there with the red hair? She has some weird connection to Lady Travesty. I don't know what, exactly.

But I'm using her as bait, see? So when we find Lady Travesty, I'll have the advantage on her.

Oh, indeed, and that bait strategy is working out well for you, is it?

It's—well—

Fortunately, there's a line of superb agents such as myself willing to take up the task and claim that reward.

After all, it's not every day you get to work for a client as rich and disreputable as GLADYS DE HARRIDAN, is it?

TWIST

Look, Chalky, if you think you're going to steal my mission and Gladys's reward, you—

All is in place, my love.

At midnight my father will breathe his last, and we elope . . . to ZANZIBAR!

Err, I think—

I think we've got the wrong partners.

Ah, yes.

Excuse me.

TWIRL!

Sham!

There's some weird stuff going on in here, Sham—someone just handed me a key to the Houses of Parliament and said the code word is "treason"?

T WIRL!

I wouldn't worry about the job, Sham. Everyone loses their touch at some point—you can't stay on top forever, can you?

I must dash now— rewards to claim, reputations to maintain, you know!

Have fun at your quadrilles—I'll give your best to Gladys!

T WIRL

I've read books, ok?

I know that when someone is emotionally distant and consistently rude, it means they have a huge secret crush on you and want to marry you and move you into their massive castle.

But I'm starting to think you might ALSO just be a DICK.

I—what books have you been reading?

FILTHY ONES!

Anyway, I'm tired of it.

Make your amazing solo plan, I don't care.

Right now I'm going to the spa to get Byron, and we're going to make our own plan to track down Lady Violet, and you can join us or you can PISS OFF.

Ok

Wait—where are you going?

I'm going to the fucking spa.

Oh, the SENSATIONAL capers James and I have been up to while you were gone, Lucy . . . I couldn't tell you any of it! I'll take it to my grave!

Please don't ask me! Please!

I can't reveal a thing! Even though it was, as I say, SENSATIONAL!

Oh, and this is James! Lord James Sponge, of the Cheltenham Sponges.

James—my co-conspirators, Lucy and Sham.

Hello, James.

Hi.

James is a feckless aristocrat avoiding military service by claiming a mysterious ailment, but he has the mind of a poet! And the body of . . .

A poet!

We've been having a WHALE of a time here. Didn't mind being left out of the adventure, no. Not. At all.

Don't worry, Byron, it wasn't all that.

False trail. Again. Dead end. Again.

But we have decided NOT to squabble about it, because we are, after all, united by a common goal.

Even though some of us haven't really done ANYTHING to help get us closer to Lady Violet.

While OTHERS are refusing to answer basic questions about why they're looking for Lady Travesty in the first place.

How did Gladys know you at the ball?

Why did Travesty leave you a note at the castle?

Who was that person you were dancing with at the quadrille?

Why were you talking to Travesty in the dungeon?

Is ANYONE going to ask me ANTHING about what I'VE been getting up to?

Any cures, cordials, mineral waters for you folks?

I couldn't help but overhear your little tiffle there.

Perhaps I may be of assistance?

Who are you?

Just a humble old gentleman with a basket full of remedies.

What kind of remedies?

Begone, quack!

Whatever you bibbling well need.

Ooh

141

SOME TIME LATER...

I say we try to get as close as possible to a potential vampire target, then one of us takes a pellet and tries to glean some information about Lady Violet's whereabouts . . .

Wait . . . where are the pellets?

Well, I took a few.

A few?

About six.

What? When? Why??

I wanted to read your minds to find out if you two are plotting anything behind my back.

You can't do that! That's so invasive!

Sham, are you hearing this?

Unbelievable. I only took three. I didn't know we could do more.

What?? Why did you do that?

Same reason. What, you mean you didn't take any?

Well, of COURSE I took a few, but only to make sure you two weren't concealing anything from ME!

Ok . . .

So we've all taken . . . quite a few of the pellets. What do we do now?

Wait for them to kick in, I suppose.

hup

UFF

WHUMP

ngh

Ummm

...Sham, is that you?

CHEEP

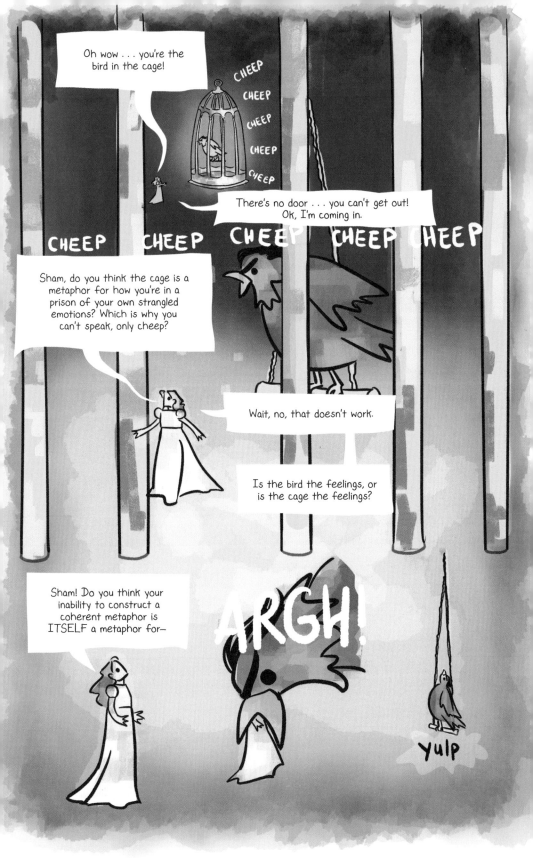

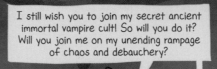

I say, chaps, I'm having a whale of a time exploring the inside of my own head. I'm fascinating!

POP!

Go away, Byron. I'm not going to be your sofa wife!

Well, I don't know what you're talking about, but I have had quite enough of you BOTH!

I'm leaving the mission—James and I are going to the club, where everyone is nice and there are no horrible GIRLS!

You'll never see me again! My memory will haunt you! I'm a notorious raaaaaaaaaaaaaaaaake

Excellent idea. To hell with this mission, I'm too good for it! See you, Lucy.

Oh, wow, Sham abandons the mission—what a shocking turn of events!

Well, enjoy your charred rabbit-for-one, I'm off to become a VAMPIRE QUEEN!

VAMPIRE TOWERS, HERE I COME!!

CHAPTER X – VAMPIRE TOWERS

SOME WEEKS LATER...

Here we go! Vampire Towers. I'm ready. So ready.

No regrets! None!

And I'm talking to myself, which is . . . probably a sign that I'm doing really well! Yes.

Helluuuu?

This better be the right castle . . .

Hello, I'm here to join the vampire cul—

Name?

Er, Lucy. I'm here to—

Place of origin?

Origin?

Where did you come from today?

Oh, er, Bath.

Lucy . . . from . . . Bath . . .

Oh no, I meant—

Follow me.

155

See, I was supposed to come here ages ago, but stuff kept getting in the way.

Anyway, I'm here now and ready to ... to ...

... What's all this?

Wait here.

Err

Excuse me ... this IS Vampires Towers, yes?

It's not a ... dance club or anything?

Yes, this is Vampire Towers! Are you visiting?

And then I turned around, and there she was!

Uh huh

I went with her straight away.

There hasn't been much opportunity for knife-throwing since then, of course . . . in fact, I've hardly seen Lady Vi since, she's so busy . . .

Come to think of it, I haven't actually left the castle since I got here.

And when was that?

Ooh, three years ago?

Right.

But I'm sure she's going to call me up for action any day now! Any day. She picked me specially, you see.

Right . . . and what about all these other girls?

Oh, them. Yes, they keep turning up . . . it's weird, they all seem to be convinced that THEY are the special ones . . . delusional, you know.

Please fill this out and turn it in when you're finished.

INDUCTION FORM FOR SECRET ANCIENT IMMORTAL VAMPIRE CLUB LTD.

I am a [circle as appropriate]:
• bored young lady
• impoverished minor aristocrat
• servant girl with ideas above her station

Seeking [circle as appropriate]:
• adventure
• scandal
• infamy
• abject violence
• thunderous sexual awakening

This can't be right.

. . . And to that effect, I shall be taking possession of your chateau on the first of the next calendar month . . .

Blah blah, death threat, declaration of supremacy, you know the rest.

Lady Violet?

Lucy! Well, this is a surprise.

Lady Travesty, there's been some mistake—

Now, my dear, have you got your form? Excellent, we can finally complete your induction!

This is the induction? A form?

Just fill that out and find yourself a little corner to settle in while it's processed. Meanwhile, there's plenty of books and bits of things to embroider and so on. You'll be spoiled for choice!

But . . . what are all these other girls doing here?

Doing?

It's just, I thought— I thought you wanted to be partners with ME.

Because I'm special.

Oh, but you ARE special, my dear! Specially suited to joining my indiscriminate mass of identical foot soldiers!

How else are we ever to outdo that sagging carcass De Harridan and her miserable band of crumbling old bores?

Gladys De Harridan?

My nemesis!

We MUST defeat her, Lucy! And you are a crucial addition, CRUCIAL! Gladys still has the edge in terms of clout, but she's falling behind!

She still recruits men, the fool. Ladies are so much more in vogue this century, especially if they are young and spirited, with a zest for rebellion, but still largely willing to obey the bounds of organized hierarchies!

But—what do you DO all day? I thought being a vampire was—you know— storming around the place, being scandalous, slashing things, cackling—

Well, we can hardly do that ALL the time, my dear.

We do a bit of slashing and cackling when the occasion calls for it—but most of the time it's just lounging around and looking imposing.

And you spirited young ladies are really ideally suited to the purpose. It's very handy to have a retinue whose idea of protest is taking a long, dramatic walk in the rain.

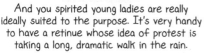
You misled me! You . . . misler!

My dear, you will admit—you never did put up a great deal of resistance . . . or even ask me any questions whatsoever. You really are exceptionally suggestible.

Oh God, you're right, I am.

So I take it Byron is on his own now, is he? Up in his castle? Good, good . . .

Oh now, you're upset. Don't worry, dear, we have plenty of ways for you to work out your frustration! How about going for a nice dramatic walk?

I will! But not because you told me to!

And don't forget to hand in your form! We'll find you a little task or two at some point, but now that you're here, there's no rush . . .

It's not as though you've got any other plans, is it . . .

I'm not suggestible! Am I?

No!

Probably?

Lucy! You made it!

Virginia?

Have a seat, old pal. Join me!

Hi, Virginia. How are you?

Not bad, not bad. Didn't think I'd be seeing you here! What happened to Sham?

We fell out.

She betrayed me, Virginia! She was going to sell me out to Gladys De Harridan! So I left!

Who? Sham? Never!

. . . Is she looking for a new sidekick?

I came here to teach her a lesson. She's not the only one with fancy vampire friends! She'll see.

Eventually.

Do you think I'm suggestible, Virginia?

Suggestible?

Like, you don't think I rely too much on the opinions of others, do you?

Nah, you're fine.

Oh, ok, phew.

You're great as you are, Lucy. You're spirited!

Really? You don't think I'm maybe, like . . . a bit ruthless and strategic, also?

Well, maybe, but not when I've been there.

Right.

162

Anyway, you've joined up now— you'll have plenty of time to work on your ruthlessness here!

Uh huh

I've got to go, though. Last-minute mission starting in a bit. Big job.

Oh yeah? A mission?

Yeah, with Lady Vi and your old poet pal, actually!

Byron? What about him?

I dunno, some plot or other. Castles, intrigue, death traps, blah blah.

A plot? To kill Byron? My Byron??

Err, that is. No. I . . . lied. That was a lie.

I'm actually doing . . . something else.

So I'm going to go do that . . . other thing.

Bye!

Urgh. What is happening.

I'm going for a walk.

How original.

Ok, this is . . . fine. Time to move on. Vampires! No more bickering, no more complications.

Right?

Oh God, you're right! I need to find Sham and save Byron—maybe I can get a message to her if I just figure out a way—maybe YOU could take it to her! If I can just attach a tiny scroll to your little bunny tail—

Wait, is that . . .

. . . Sham?

What is she
doing . . .?

Psst, Sham!

AAHH

ARGH,
don't shoot!

SWING

LUCY!

What the hell are you
doing? I could have
shot you!

That's why I said
don't shoot!

You don't think it'd be wiser
to shout that
from a distance?

If I'd shouted it from a
distance, you may have
misheard and shot me!

I . . . what are you doing out here?

What are YOU doing out here? Don't lie!

You're not still after Lady Travesty, are you? Cos there's a lot of very bored young ladies with pent-up aggression in that castle. You wouldn't last very long.

No. What? No . . . I abandoned the quest. Really. I'm not working for Gladys anymore.

Oh, ok.

So . . .

I came to say sorry, for being rude and for double-crossing you. I'm sorry. And I also came . . . to ask for your help.

Help?

I got wind of some plot to kill Byron.

Yeah, I heard about that.

Thought we'd better go save him.

I thought you were better at doing these things on your own.

Well. Yes. But.

But?

I dunno, Luce. It's odd. Ever since we fell out in Bath . . . it's like I've been unwell. I've had this strange painful feeling, right here. Where my heart is. Like it was damaged or something. Not working properly. Malfunctioning.

Not . . . intact.

Broken?

Yeah, exactly!

166

And you know how your thoughts are usually about food and weaponry and stuff? Ever since then, all I think about is you! And Byron. And even that weird French bird.

Anyway, it's troubling.

I think it's pretty common, actually.

Really? Other people get it?

Constantly.

Well, they should warn people about it! Write it down or something, share it around . . . explain the feeling so others will understand what's happening . . . publish it in volumes or something . . .

Maybe make it rhyme, so it's easy to remember? Kind of like a poem?

Yeah, good idea!

Aw, Sham.

Oh

Ok!

So . . . want to come save Byron with me? Wait, you're not a vampire already, are you?

Nah, I never handed my form in. But maybe we can be a bit less ruthless and strategic this time.

How about from now on we're just nice to each other?

Ok, how about from now on I'll be nice to you and you be the same with me.

Except the bit where you're secretly plotting to join a vampire cult.

I was always nice to you.

Ok!

Ok, ok, you don't have to go on about it.

167

So she's just got a castle full of women?

Yeah, she seems to collect them.

She said it was something about outdoing Gladys De Harridan? I didn't get exactly how, though.

Weird.

Anyway, when's this carriage coming?

We need to get to Byron's club and get him out before Lady Travesty works out where he is.

Don't worry, I think I see her now.

Her?

*clop clop clop cl

Good evening, my urchins!

Ready for another adventure?

169

Err

Just a tick, BB!

SHAM, what on Earth? Don't you remember where BB's last few tips have landed us?

Keep your voice down!

Ok, so she's a bit . . . scattergun . . . but she was driving this way anyway and offered us a ride!

I dunno how else you thought we'd get to London on time with no money. Not everyone has a giant magic bird handy.

Yeah, I wonder where Napoleon is . . .

> MEANWHILE... <

I used to own France, you know.

Oui, oui, chérie.

Sacrebleu!

Marie-Thérèse!

BAM

GASP

Je vous challenge, Monsieur!

PAF

uf

Don't you think it's odd that she's always so keen to help and yet every time we end up in more trouble than when we started?

cooo-eee!

And all those dead husbands . . . and she's so CHEERFUL all the time! It's suspicious!

Ok, let's just get to London. First sign of trouble, we leg it.

Fine.

Ready, BB!

Come along, darlings!

SOME TIME LATER...

Ok, girls, follow me.

No, BB, we've been through this before—it's a gentlemen's club. They won't let—

You there, doorman!

Baroness De Bri!

I have come to retrieve my late husband's dentures, which he misplaced.

Misplaced?

In the sandwich he was attempting to eat.

Certainly, Baroness, and may I say what a pleasure it is to see you looking so well, following your husband's tragic altercation with that antique ice pick—

You may NOT! Stand aside!

HRK

SWISH

Wow, that was easy.

What's a sand witch?

Walter, what are you doing in London?

Is Byron here?

Byron had to depart to Scotland, for a rendezvous with . . . Madame Fortune.

Who's that? Is that another vampire lady?

There's TOO many of them!

Foolish girl! Isn't it obvious? Lady Travesty and I conspired against you!

She desired a castle and new recruits. I desired Byron's downfall. Together we concocted a LABYRINTHINE plot that united our twin goals!

And you fell for it! You attended the ball with the baroness, didn't you?

Yes?

And I'll bet you Byron decided to wear a huge, attention-seeking outfit, didn't he?

He did.

And I'll bet he even got his sword out and waved it around.

God dammit

Wait—so your plan was to make Byron go to a ball? What? Explain more!

To attend the ball . . . and ensure his DOWNFALL!

COMMENCE FLASHBACK!

But, wait, I still don't get it. Why did you send him to the vampire ball? So he would cause a scene and they'd kill him?

Not just kill him. DESTROY him!

Reputation is everything in this business! I can only surmise that Byron's popularity is owed to the fact that his audience is ignorant of his insalubrious exploits. They must be enlightened!

So—he goes to the ball, and the newspapers report that he died fighting at a debauched demimonde gathering, exposing his dissolute lifestyle once and for all! His legacy destroyed!

I mean—who wants to read the poems of a reckless cad who spends all his time fighting duels and seducing women? What kind of culture would venerate a character like that?

He will be discredited and forgotten! And who, then, will be remembered as the greatest, sexiest, popular-est poet of the era?

WALTER SCOTT.

Byron will be ruined! I shall be the KING OF ROMANCE!

AHAHAHAHAAA!

Right, so he's obviously lost it.

HA HA HA HA HA HA

Lucy, get hold of Napoleon and let's get the hell up to Scotland and fix this mess.

Ok, I'll give it a go.

Come on, Napoleon, where are you . . .

Lady Travesty is not the only one with a lust for property and a talent for HAREBRAINED scheming . . . it just so happens that I MYSELF have laid a trap for the trap! Lady Travesty is certainly now on her way to deal with Byron at his castle. What she is unaware of, however, is that my men arrived there first and have hidden alchemical explosives all around the castle's foundations! Travesty will arrive, and she and Byron will be blown to kingdom come!

Very neat, n'est-ce pas?

So, miss Lucy, I am afraid we must detain you and your diminutive friend while all that is sorted out.

You do have a knack for inserting yourselves where you are not needed.

No chance, Gladys!

BB—what's French for "Go fuck yourself?"

Vas te faire foutre?

What she said.

Actually, in this case you're addressing your social superiour, so the formal "Allez vous faire foutre" is probably more appropriate.

I tire of this. Seize them!

You're going to kill us?

No, your little band has ruined enough of my carpets.

Find a dungeon somewhere to throw them in.

Baroness—thank you for your service, you may go. Out of delicacy and good sportsmanship, I will allow you to take a moment . . . to rub it in their faces.

BB, you rat!

Oh, girls! I don't know what to say.

Why, BB? Why did you betray us? Was it for money?

Money? How could you think that? I can't have failed to demonstrate that I am already incommodiously rich!

Then what was it? What was your plan?

Plan? Err, well . . . you will keep this to yourselves, but the truth is . . . gosh, this is embarrassing . . . I really did think I was doing you a good turn! I don't know where Gladys is getting all this "service" stuff.

I suppose I haven't really been paying attention. But you will admit the dynamics of this community are rather baroque! I think this is what you would call an unfortunate coincidence.

But . . . what about all the murdered husbands, then? You can't deny that one!

Oh no, I'll own up to that, absolutely. How else is a girl to make a living?

Besides, I can write my little outings with you dears off as charity work, so it's good business too. For the expenses and so forth.

HNGHHH

Charity work?

179

Oh, I do hate to see you vexed. I feel quite awful about it . . .

. . . But I'm afraid I must dash—that Walter Scott is looking rather rich and unbalanced these days . . . very much my type, as it were . . . I'm going to see if he needs a lift home.

BB, you can't leave us!

Terribly sorry, darlings! Best of luck!

Now, my dears, I hope you like LANGUISHING, because you're in for a—

SMASH

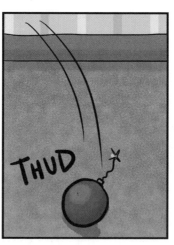
THUD

What on—

la bombe

Lucy, DUCK!

BOOM

Castle! What happened?

Miss Lucy, how good to see you.

Castle, has anyone been here? Is Byron here? We heard that there were—

Lord Byron did have some visitors. A rather unruly lot.

Unruly?

Running all over the place, hiding in corners . . .

. . . Rummaging around in cellars . . .

Rummaging?

Rummaging, miss.

That'll be the explosives!

Castle, we're—you're— in danger! They're going to blow you up!

Oh my, how tiresome.

Castle, you need to help us look for the explosives—where's Byron?

In his room, miss. He's been there for days.

He told me not to bother tidying up, something about how life is futile and there's no point to anything and that he was going to stay in bed for the rest of his life.

184

185

186

187

Phew

Think this is a safe distance?

Yeah, we'll be fine.

I can't believe Gladys even CAME here. She's the one who rigged the castle to blow up!

I don't think logic is their strong point, Luce.

Better go find Byron, I suppose.

I liked your poem.

Thanks.

Don't tell Byron about it, will you?

Sure.

It's just . . . he looks up to me as this strong, silent, heroic type. I wouldn't want to shatter his illusions, you know?

Don't worry.

... and then JAMES said he would write to me, but he HASN'T, and I don't know whether to write first, cos what if HIS letter is already on its way to me and it's too late to change what I said in MY letter—

Yesss, yessss, tell me more, Byron, MORE!

NO, Gwendolyne, stop that!

Shoo!

Hrghhh

What happened? Did the vampires come for me?

They did, actually. But they're now otherwise engaged. I think we're safe.

Oh good.

Hi, Sham, how are you?

Fine. You?

Yep, fine.

Cool.

Well, I haven't heard any explosions.

Shall we go look?

195

Ever since we had that chat, Lucy, I've been thinking of you all, and I just HATED the idea of you being blown to bits. So I came up here with Lady Vi and was sneaking around the castle, and I heard you mention explosives, so I thought—here's a chance to prove my loyalty to the team!

So I searched all over the castle, and I found the explosives in the whiskey cellar!

Also I managed to rescue a few bottles.

Good SHOW, old chap!

And what about Gladys and Lady Violet? Are they still fighting?

Hmm, dunno.

I saw a lot of blood and guts in the hallway, though, so they might have stabbed each other and dissolved, you know how they do.

They get together for a pitched battle every few years, I think—a show of dominance to remind each other and all the other vampires who's boss. They'll be back at it in no time, I'm sure.

Why would they do that?!

Well, they're immortal, they have to fill the time somehow, I suppose. Nothing like a harebrained scheme to enliven things!

And when I say enliven, I mean metaphorically, as they are, technically, still dead.

So . . . it was all for nothing? All that? We were just caught up in a squabble between two old biddies and a deranged poet?

I say!

She means Walter Scott.

Ah

Not nothing Lucy—look at us! Thanks to them, we've formed a proper little gang! I can just picture the scrapes we're going to get into.

Sham knows I'm a valuable team member! Always two steps ahead.

Wait—Virginia, you found the explosives in the whiskey cellar?

Yes, sir!

And did you disarm them before you left?

Ah

SOME TIME LATER...

So! What now?

Well, I need to get back to work. Make some money somehow. I'm definitely on the vampires' blacklist now.

I'll have to find some other rich criminal enterprise to employ me.

Werewolves?

I'm thinking the British government.

Tell you what—I'm looking forward to some non-vampire company.

Awfully self-involved, vampires. Only ever talk about themselves, you know?

You're absolutely right, Virginia.

I SHALL write to James! Dash the consequences! Less hideous far the tempest's roar than ne'er to brave the billows more!

Better to sink beneath the shock than moulder piecemeal on the rock! I say, that's rather good . . .

199

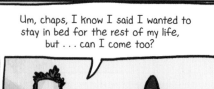

Um, chaps, I know I said I wanted to stay in bed for the rest of my life, but . . . can I come too?

LIKEWISE, chaps, I'm ready to pledge my skills to the group!

I've lost my sword, and I'm a bit tired, and I don't like taking directions or compromising or doing anything that will require me to pay attention for longer than ten minutes at a time, but otherwise I think I could be a really invaluable team asset!

Ok! Four people.

That's fine. Four.

Ok, then.

That will be . . . fine.

What about Castle? Is it going to be ok?

It's weathered worse, haven't you, old girl?

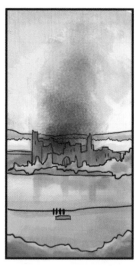

Ah, the silent treatment! No less than I deserve. It'll be back on form in no time, you'll see.

RIGHT, come hither, Napoleon! We must fly!

No?

That's fine!

In your own time.

Perhaps if we started to walk in the general direction of adventure . . .

What if we get lost?

You won't get lost.

Not if you're with me.

WOOP!

Oh, ok . . . except . . . except you did say that once before . . .

We've got no supplies except whiskey and sweets.

Byron's still in his nightie.

Come along, old boy! Don't worry about all that!

Onward!

Onward to ADVENTURE!

Acknowledgments

Thanks to Rebekah Rarely, Heather Flaherty, Melissa Zahorsky, Siân Docksey, Zeba Clarke, and Michael McGovern for their support, hard work, and invaluable advice in the making of this book.

Thanks also to Leo, Aisling, Agnes, Jenny, Alice, Lucie, Shabnam, Léa, Jasper, Fliss, and Jessica for coming to my rescue at one time or another, and to Norma, Ed, Patrick, and Michael for absolutely everything.

About the Author

Emily McGovern grew up in Brussels and writes bios for herself in the third person cos it looks way more professional. She graduated from University College London in 2014 with a degree in Russian Studies. She now works as a full-time cartoonist and is the creator of the webcomic *My Life as a Background Slytherin*. This is her first graphic novel.